UMBRELLA IN TIME

By
LESLEY JEPPS

Facebook   By Lesley Jepps
Instagram Lesley_Jepps_childrens_author

UMBRELLA IN TIME
BY LESLEY JEPPS

To the reader. What do we know about time? Is it possible that the past, present or future can exist together, or that there may be somewhere where time does not exist at all?

UMBRELLA IN TIME
BY LESLEY JEPPS

CONTENTS

LESLEY JEPPS   <u>SYNOPSIS OF UMBRELLA IN TIME</u>

Umbrella in Time is a children's novel for 8yrs + about a girl called Rachel, who finds a Victorian Umbrella in her father's office. It takes her back in time to the Second World War, and then to Victorian Liverpool, where she meets previous owners of the umbrella, who are linked to her family in the present. In a series of adventures, she travels through time, to find a missing ruby necklace which will help her father, whose firm is going bankrupt. A future owner of the umbrella finally appears, to solve the mystery. Will the Umbrella give up its secret?

CHAPTER ONE

A SURPRISE FIND

"That looks old!" gasped Rachel, peering inside her dad's office cupboard. She had just dropped off his lunch, which he'd forgotten that morning. Nothing escaped her notice and he sighed.

"I thought you were meeting a friend and going for a swim? You should be enjoying the summer holidays. He got up wearily from his computer. "Go on then, what have you seen?"

Rachel had already made a grab for the dusty object, which she opened, straight into his chest. "Sorry dad," she laughed, "but this is great."

"It's an umbrella, Rachel," he snapped. "It's been there for years. No-one uses it. Now I need peace to work. Go for a swim."

"But it looks old," she answered, undeterred. The green waxed silk covering glowed against the ribs and black stem. "It might be Victorian. Take it and go," he ordered.

"Thanks dad. See ya later." He looked tired and gaunt and she'd felt the tension at home recently. No-one told her anything. A shadow crossed her face, but she fell silent and left him to it.

Outside, she bumped into her mum laden with bags.

"Are you okay?" she asked.

"I need help with these, love. My car wouldn't start this morning and I got the bus in. Take this heavy one would you."

Rachel held the bag in one hand and the umbrella in the other. "Where did you get that?" asked Mrs. Denvers, looking beyond it to the writing on the wall behind, which read DENVERS CONSTRUCTION.

"In dad's office cupboard," she replied, following her mother's gaze. "What's wrong mum? You and dad are acting strange."

Her mum focused. "Everything's fine, we need to get home." She brushed a hand across her white face and smiled. It didn't reach her eyes. Rachel wasn't going to push it, so she took another bag, balanced the umbrella inside, and walked down to the bus stop round the corner.

Later, after helping at home, she dashed out down the road with the umbrella, to the antique shop in the high street and the man told Rachel that the umbrella was indeed Victorian as her father had suggested.

"Made around 1860," he said, scratching his head with his bony fingers. "The ribs are made of whalebone, the handle's ebony, but a lot of similar umbrellas were made at that time, so it isn't an antique of much value." He did add that the color of the covering was unusual.

"Cheers," said Rachel, who was thrilled with it anyway. Her friend Linda thought it was "cool" when she showed it off at the leisure centre.

That evening, her dad came in from work looking grey and ill. "We're bankrupt, Irene," he said, weakly. "My firm's finished."

"I know," she sighed.

"How?" he asked, astonished.

"I knew the men had been on strike too long and wouldn't be able to catch up on the work. You can`t keep everything from me." She put her arm around her husband's shoulders, while Rachel sat stunned at a nearby table. At least now she knew what was wrong. She felt helpless.

"We'll have to sell the house, won't we dad?"

"I'm afraid so Rachel. I'll ring the estate agent in the morning."

Her world felt less secure.

Later, in her room, she let her gaze travel over the familiar objects she knew so well. The wooden chest of drawers on which lay her mobile phone; the fitted pine wardrobe and bookshelf and her unicorn lampshade. She made a quick call to Linda, telling her the bad news, then pressed the power off button and sat down on the bed next to the umbrella.. "I wonder what happened to the people who owned you?" she asked, half wondering. As though in answer, the umbrella began to vibrate then spin, while the familiar objects disappeared and her bathrobe transformed into a different outfit altogether.

CHAPTER TWO

THE GIRL IN THE UNDERGROUND

Wide eyed with shock, Rachel absorbed her new surroundings. Beneath her feet, was a railway platform, filled with people, lying in bunks or drinking tea or coffee out of flasks. Shaded lights hung from the curved roof, and there were no windows. Her clothes made her gasp. She was wearing a green and yellow gymslip and green cardigan and gabardine, and on her feet were black shoes and short socks. Looking up, she glimpsed the railway lines below the platform and a sign on the wall which said 'Oxford Circus', and it finally dawned where she was. 'The London Underground,' she thought, puzzled. Far above her head, she could hear explosions, which made her doubt her sanity. Either that, or she was dreaming. She turned round and caught sight of herself in a mirror. "My hair!" she wailed. "What's the matter with your hair?" asked a cheeky boy in a black cap and blazer, standing jauntily a few feet away. "It used to be long and curly," cried Rachel, "and now it's short and straight." People began to move restlessly under their blankets. "Your hair looks fine to me, dear," said a plump woman beside her. "That's a popular style for the girls today. "You've forgotten you had it cut, no doubt." She smiled sympathetically.

"No, you don't understand," said Rachel, frantically. "I was in my bedroom at home a few minutes ago, and now I find that I'm here with you. I'm dressed in different clothes and with a different hairstyle."

"Had a knock on the head and gone batty, have you?" sneered the boy, planting his feet wide. "We all have to take shelter down here when there's an air raid. What's the matter with you?"

"Watch your manners, Jeremy," said the plump woman angrily, "or I'll give you a thick ear." Then turning to Rachel, she said sweetly, "are you alright, love? I think you ought to see a doctor if you've lost your memory."

"What year is this?" asked Rachel, ignoring the woman.

"Why, it's October, 1940," she answered, puzzled. "The Germans have been bombing London day and night since the seventh of September." She paused, to alter her sitting position on the cold stone floor. "We'll never surrender though," she continued, with a distant look in her eyes. "We'll put up a good fight to save our islands from Nazi rule."

"I'll second that," said Jeremy, looking straight at Rachel, who was sitting motionless in a daze. 'I've been brought back in time to the second world war,' she thought, stupefied. 'Is it possible?' Then she remembered the umbrella spinning in her bedroom. 'Could the umbrella have brought me here?' she murmured to herself.

"Did you speak dear?" asked the plump woman, who was by now wondering if she should find a red cross nurse further down the platform.

"No, I was just thinking," replied Rachel. "Please don't worry."

"Well if you say so," said the woman doubtfully. Rachel stood up and began to walk away, as the woman heaved herself to her feet and lumbered up behind her to put a short stubby hand on her arm. "Perhaps you should stay with us. You don't look too well," she said.

"No, really," said Rachel, looking around anxiously for an escape route. "I'm fine."

"Oh let her go, mum," snapped Jeremy. She's a bit queer in the head." His mother shrugged philosophically and turned away, while Rachel retreated to the far end of the station. She hadn't been there long, when the boy came plodding after her with a cardboard box under his arm. "Here, you forgot this," he said, thrusting it into her lap.

"What is it?" asked Rachel, alarmed.

"Your gas mask," he answered, disgustedly.

For a while, she listened to the sound of the bombing outside and the heavy breathing of people sleeping nearby, as she tried to remember what she'd learnt about the war in London from her history books at school. She knew there would be no trains in the evening, as people only slept in the underground stations at night, and the all clear siren would sound when the bombing stopped. She lifted the lid of the cardboard box to examine the mask inside, and found that it was just like the pictures she had seen of them at school. There was a single eye-piece made from a substance called mica, and the metal filter near the mouth, purified the air that was breathed in. The mask itself was made of rubber, and three straps held it on the head. She hoped she wouldn't have to use it. Her eyes were drooping and she felt quite tired, but she couldn't help thinking about her parents and whether they had missed her. "I must find the umbrella," she murmured. "If it did bring me here, it can take me back." She asked someone the time and he told her it was 5.30, not long before dawn. A poster on the wall caught her attention. 'Leave the children where they are, Mother' it said. 'In the countryside for safety,' thought Rachel, as her eyes closed, and she began to sink slowly sideways towards a blanket on the floor. Her eyes focused dimly on the people around her--- a man in a dirty cloth cap, snoring loudly; a black-haired woman, combing her hair, and a girl of her own age sitting between two men. The girl was staring vacantly at nothing in particular, and she held something green. Rachel's eyes closed. Suddenly, she was wide awake. She gazed more intently at the girl, who had short brown hair. In between her feet, lay Rachel's green umbrella!

The all clear siren began to wail monotonously, and the station became alive with people. They climbed out of bunks and stampeded towards the exits. She looked over to where the girl had been sitting and saw only a sea of faces. Several yards ahead, she made out a flash of green and a curly head of

hair, as she pushed her way through the tightly packed
crowd, to the street above. "It's pitch black out here. Where
are the street lights?" cried Rachel, involuntarily, before
remembering the black-out restrictions described in her school
history lessons. Glancing around in panic, she saw not far
ahead, the green covering of the umbrella, glowing in the dark
between the lights of dim torches. Letting out a sigh of relief,
she began to follow behind.

At first, there were quite a few people all going in the same
direction, but one by one, they went their separate ways,
calling out to each other in the night. Now there was only the
girl she was following, who quickened her pace and crossed a
road, making it difficult to keep up. Several vehicles with
shuttered headlamps, drove past in rapid succession, and as
Rachel turned a corner, the girl had disappeared. She was
alone in the darkness.

CHAPTER THREE

LOST AND FOUND

The sky lightened, and for a few moments the road was quiet, until heavy footsteps echoed from behind. Her mouth went dry and her heart raced as a dim torch was shone directly into her face.

"Hello there," said a friendly masculine voice. "What are you doing out here at this time? You should be tucked up in a shelter. Where do you live?"

Rachel became flustered. "I----I don't know," she answered, hesitantly, digging her fingers into her palms.

"You don't know!" exclaimed the man, surprised. "Were you out here while the air raid was on?" Without waiting for an answer, he continued. "You seem shocked. What's your name?"

"Rachel," she answered, truthfully. "Are you an air raid warden?" She'd seen the A.R.P. letters on his helmet.

"Yes," he answered, looking at Rachel strangely. "You are a funny one and no mistake. Have you got any papers or documents which might identify you?"

"No."

"Well then," he continued, philosophically. "I'll take you to a reception centre and let them sort you out. I need some sleep."

"What's a reception centre?"

It's a place where people go when their homes have been bombed and they have nowhere to live." He put his arm through Rachel's and propelled her along the street in the direction from which he had come.

'He's probably had quite a night of it,' she thought, seeing his stern profile and tired looking eyes. Her history book was coming alive for her, and she was actually living in the past!

She knew she couldn't tell him the truth though, as he would never believe her.

They reached the end of the street, and on a wall, she could make out a sign which said 'Ashdown Road.' The edge of the kerb was painted black and white and she realized that it had helped her get across the road when she was following the girl with the green umbrella. She was trapped in time.

The scene changed drastically in the next street, as a screaming woman ran out of a burning house. The fire lit up her anguished face and she fell to her knees in despair, shouting, "someone save my husband!"

"Stay here and don't move, Rachel," said the warden, abruptly. "I'll have to deal with this."

Rachel stood transfixed, vaguely hearing him speak. Several men ran into the burning building, but the intense heat drove them back. The woman sobbed as the warden led her into the arms of a friend who held her tight.

"Was her husband in the house?" asked Rachel, quietly.

"Yes," he replied. He took off his helmet with a large dirty hand and wiped the sweat off his forehead.

"I'm sorry, what happens now?"

"Her friend will look after her," answered the warden, bluntly. "It's the war. Come on love," he said, wearily. Rachel took his outstretched arm and they walked on again down the street, passing black out curtains at the windows; lamp posts painted black and white; shattered buildings half standing; rubble; water tanks standing on waste ground and sandbags lying outside important buildings.

At last, they reached the centre, outside a converted dance hall, and the warden led Rachel to a row of seats. At the front of the hall was a long table, behind which were sitting a number of women. Above their heads hung placards displaying the words 'Billeting,' 'Evacuation' and 'Travel vouchers.'

"Elsie's free now, Rachel," said the warden, suddenly. He pointed to a vacant chair in front of a thin-faced woman with dark hair and glasses. "She'll know what to do with you."

"You seem to know everyone around here," said Rachel, amazed. "Are they all so helpful?"

The warden laughed and his eyes crinkled. "The war brings people together."

"I suppose it does," she said, thoughtfully.

The thin woman looked searchingly at Rachel, and was puzzled. "She doesn't appear to be like the people we get in here suffering from shock, Jack. She looks alert and full of life." Then, adjusting her glasses, she said, "I'll take care of her anyway. You go home."

"Thanks, Elsie," said the warden, relieved. "I'll leave you now, Rachel. Goodbye."

"Bye, and thanks," said Rachel, warmly. She watched him leave, then turned and obeyed Elsie's instructions to sit and read for a while, until she had made some enquiries.

"Someone is bound to come searching for you if you stay here," she said. Rachel knew they wouldn't. She suddenly felt alone and frightened. She couldn't stay here, yet she felt she couldn't get away either. Elsie was watching. Somehow, she had to find the girl with the umbrella. The umbrella had the answer, she was sure of it. She looked at all the people sitting in rows behind her, and caught sight of the notice . 'careless talk costs lives.' She would have to wait.

The day passed slowly, starting with a voluntary worker handing out small rations for breakfast and dinner. Rachel ate hungrily. By tea time, she was beginning to wonder if she could walk out unseen, when the door opened, and in walked a plump woman in a thick dark blue coat and hat. Standing by her side, was a girl in a brown gabardine, dripping water all over the floor. Rachel sat bolt upright with surprise. In the girl's hand, was the green umbrella.

CHAPTER FOUR
AN EXCITING DISCOVERY

"Evening Elsie," said the plump woman, brightly. "Dreadful weather out there. We've brought some extra food for the children."

"Thanks Doris, and you too, Emily," said Elsie. "We've quite a crowd in here tonight and they could do with a bit of cheering up. I don't know what we'd do without you."

"Glad to help," said Doris, laughing. Her good humour lifted the spirits and people smiled. Emily gave out rations, while the umbrella swung to and fro over her arm. Rachel took her opportunity, and picked up her gas mask. "Hello," she said, pleasantly.

"Oh hello," said the girl, turning round to face her. "I'm Emily. Who are you?

Rachel introduced herself. "Where do you get the extra food?"

"I come in here every night. We grow our own vegetables in a patch in the back garden, and trade the surplus for other types of rations. Was your home bombed last night?"

She hesitated. "No – or at least I don't know. I can't remember."

"Can't you remember anything?" exclaimed Emily, her brown eyes opening wide.

"I remember seeing you in the underground station at Oxford Circus this morning," said Rachel. "I was attracted by your green umbrella. It reminded me of something."

"How strange," said the girl, thoughtfully. "I'd been to see a friend last night and coming home, I was caught in the air raid and dashed down to the underground." She studied Rachel seriously for a few seconds. "Why don't you come home with us for tea?

We could tell Elsie where you're going, then if anyone comes looking for you, she knows where you are."

"I'd love to," said Rachel, pleased. "But hadn't you better ask your mum first?"

"I'm sure she would love to have you," laughed Emily.

 Her mum was quite happy when asked, and she put a large plump arm around Rachel's shoulders. "Poor love. I'm sure you'll remember soon. You come home with us."

"Thank you," gasped Rachel, almost crushed.

"Bye Mrs Hanson," shouted a lady in a black coat.

"Bye," she replied, with a wave.

'Is there a connection?' thought Rachel, surprised. She'd heard her father mention the name Hanson.

Outside, it was dark and the rain had turned to drizzle. Mrs. Hanson put up her umbrella, and Emily shared the green one with Rachel. They walked for some time, listening to Mrs. Hanson's tales of work in a munitions factory, while Emily rolled her eyes. She'd heard it all before. Eventually, they turned into Ashdown Road and took the second turning right into Tennyson Avenue.   The Hanson's house was number six and it had two long sash windows upstairs and two downstairs. Mr. Hanson got up from his chair when they entered, and extended a hard calloused hand. He said "hello," rather wearily and Rachel was drawn to his deep sorrowful eyes.

"Well," said Mrs. Hanson, brightly. "I'll make tea." She disappeared into the kitchen, while Rachel followed Emily up to her bedroom with growing excitement. She felt certain she was close to an important discovery, and wanted to know all she could of the Hansons. "What does your father do for a living, Emily?" she asked.

"He was a builder," she replied. Rachel tensed. There could be a connection to her father, but in what way?

"Of course, he's not a builder now," continued Emily, sadly. "The government stopped all building work because of the bombing. He works in a factory like my mum now."

"Have you any brothers and sisters?"

"Yes, one brother. He's a fighter pilot with the R.A.F."

"That must be hard for you."

"I try not to think about his job. Sit on my bed if you like. I need to hang up some clothes." Rachel glanced round at the heavy oak dressing table and long mirror, the black out curtains and the brass bed-stead. On the floor lay the green umbrella. "It's a lovely room," said Rachel, keeping her eye on the green silk folds. Her elbow knocked a photo frame on a bedside table, and she caught it just in time. "Sorry Emily. Is the man in the photo a relative?"

"His name was Michael Drew," she replied, sadly. "He was an old friend of my dad's. We nursed him here while he was ill, until he died last month. He slept in this room on my bed, while I slept on the settee downstairs."

Rachel shuddered and got up quickly from the bed. "Is that why your dad looks so down?"

"He misses him a lot," she replied. "Michael had a great sense of humour, and was kind. He inherited five ruby necklaces from his great-great-grandmother, which were worth a fortune. The fifth went missing in Victorian times. When he became ill, he made a will leaving them to my mum and dad, and he kept it on the cabinet by this bed. Michael was the only one of his family left and he never married, and as he knew that my dad had a dream to start his own building firm after the war, he left them to him in the will. We were his family." She paused and looked down at the floor. "The green umbrella had been in his family for many generations, and he gave me that as well. It belonged originally to the daughter of his great-great-grandparents in the 1860's.

Rachel was stunned. "Where are the necklaces now?" she asked.

"That's the trouble. We couldn't find the will when Michael died. Dad asked him where he wanted to put it for safe keeping, and he said that he would sleep on it. Michael was always joking."

"How did it disappear from the cabinet?"

"A solicitor friend came to see him one day, and we thought he'd taken it."

"Had he?" asked Rachel, spellbound.

"No," sighed Emily. "We've looked everywhere, but it's vanished into thin air. Dad is more depressed over his death than the loss of the will, but mum and I wanted him to have the necklaces. We don't know where they are either. Michael never told us where he'd put them. I suppose the will would explain everything."

They each became silent, lost in their own thoughts, while a clock chimed in the hall below.

"Tea, girls!" shouted Mrs. Hanson, breaking the spell. Rachel's instincts were to grab the umbrella and hope she would wake up from the dream, but her arm was taken, and she was pulled downstairs. After they had eaten, Mr. Hanson went out on A.R.P. duties and Emily and her mum took Rachel back to the rehabilitation centre. Emily told Rachel that they would see her the next day at tea-time, if she was still there.

"I'll sleep on it," he'd said. Rachel stilled. 'It's in the mattress!' She jumped up and ran past the people asleep on the floor and out into the faint light which heralded the dawn, feeling no fear, only exhilaration. Into Ashdown Road she ran, then second right into Tennyson Avenue. A long whistle sounded somewhere above her head and a loud explosion ripped the night. The force of the blast threw her against a wall, and for a few minutes, she lay dazed. Eventually, she dragged herself to her feet and looked across the road. Number six had received a direct hit!

CHAPTER FIVE
REVELATIONS

Stunned and shaking, she walked along a passageway beside the one remaining wall and into the back garden. At the end, to one side of the vegetable patch, there was a domed roof of earth sunk partly into the ground. The front was made of corrugated iron and it had a small door, through which she saw Emily and her parents. Weak with relief, she was about to hurry over, when she saw how silent and still they were. A glistening tear slid down Emily's cheek as she looked at the remains of her home, then she turned and saw Rachel.

"What are you doing here?" she exclaimed. Mrs. Hanson bustled across and gave her a bear hug, while Mr. Hanson looked at her dismally.
"I'm sorry you've lost your home. Thank goodness you're all safe," she blurted. Then her mind cleared. "Has your mattress been burnt too, Emily?"
"No, we brought it down to the shelter after Michael died, so we had something to sleep on. Why?"
"I think Michael put the will inside it."
They all gasped, then sprang into action. "Get the mattress," said Mr. Hanson, at last showing some sign of life, and all four stumbled down the steps. A masked torch lay on the ground, together with some provisions and water. On one of the bunks lay the green umbrella, and Rachel gave thanks to whatever power had preserved it. First Emily, then her mum, and finally her dad, examined the mattress for any sign of a tear, without success. Then Rachel offered. Again, nothing. The tension mounted as they felt the rough fabric.
"I don't think it's here," sighed Emily.
"Nice try anyway Rachel," said Mrs. Hanson, disappointed.
"You're sure this is Michael's mattress?" asked Rachel, puzzled.

"We're sure," said Emily.

Rachel sighed. "The light isn't all that good in here yet. Let's use the torch, we might have missed it."

"That's true," replied Mrs. Hanson. "We probably all got in each other's way last time, too." The Hansons peered over Rachel's shoulder as she moved the beam of the torch inch by inch across the surface. They came to the end of one side. Nothing. The mattress was turned over and Rachel began again. Not a thing. Then, on the last corner, they found a neat row of stitching.

"I don't believe it!" gasped Mrs. Hanson, amazed.

"It doesn't mean there's a will in there though," said Emily, doubtfully.

"Who's going to undo the stitching to find out?" asked Rachel, brightly. Mrs. Hanson looked her straight in the eye. "You are."

"I'll get the scissors," said Mr. Hanson, quietly.

Rachel took the scissors from his outstretched hand, and hoped that her theory was right. They would be crushed again if she wasn't. She began to cut each stitch carefully, and as the fabric opened, she put her hand underneath. Her fingers probed, while three pairs of eyes watched her every move. At last they came into contact with something smooth and crackly.

"I think I've got it!" she cried, pulling out a long brown envelope sealed with a piece of red wax.

"That certainly looks like Michael's will," gasped Emily.

"Will you open it love" said Mrs. Hanson, stunned.

Rachel nodded, then pulled at the seal without success.

"Here, let me try," said Emily, using all her strength.

"Give it to me Emily," demanded Mrs. Hanson, but after a few minutes, even she gave up. "You try John," she said, handing it over.

Mr. Hanson put his fingers on the seal and pulled. At last, it came open, and he handed it back to his wife to read, the sorrow now gone from his eyes. Mrs. Hanson took out two sheets of white printed paper and a small silver key fell out and dropped on to the floor.

She bent down to pick it up and looked at the others in surprise. The atmosphere was electric.

"This will is made by me, MICHAEL DREW," read Mrs. Hanson, hesitantly. Then more boldly. "I devise and bequeath my four ruby necklaces to John Hanson and his wife Doris Hanson. The necklaces will be found in a deposit box, number 312 at the Metropolitan Bank on North Street, West London. The key is enclosed herewith." Mrs. Hanson stopped reading and put the will into her husband's hands with the key.

"Dear Michael," said Mr. Hanson, softly.

"Thanks Rachel," said Emily.

"Thanks love," said Mrs. Hanson, warmly. "We can never repay you for this."

"I'm just glad it was there," said Rachel. "I suppose we'll have to go back to the reception centre now."

They all nodded sadly and went outside to pick their way through the rubble of their old house. Emily disappeared, saying she would look for anything usable, leaving Rachel holding the green umbrella. Suddenly, it wrenched out of her grasp and spun madly on the floor, while the scene changed yet again.

Relief at last. She was in her bedroom at home, and the umbrella was on the bed. 'I've been away for a day and a night,' she thought in amazement. 'Mum and dad will be crazy.' Then she glanced at the alarm clock, which showed that no time had passed in her absence. A knock on the door made her jump. "Are you in bed, Rachel?" asked her mother. She hesitated for a few seconds, then dived between the covers.

"Yes mum, come in,"

Her mother entered, dressed as Rachel had last seen her, and walked over to the bed to tuck in the bedclothes.

"Goodnight love," she said, kissing Rachel warmly.

"Goodnight mum." Her arms reached up to give her a hug.
"You are affectionate tonight," laughed Mrs. Denvers.
"Anyone would think you hadn't seen me for days, instead of
a few minutes ago. Go to sleep now, and try to forget
everything." She opened the door and was gone, leaving
Rachel in the darkness.

'Time has stood still here,' she thought, hazily, as she drifted
off to sleep.

In the morning, after breakfast, Rachel followed her dad into
the living room.

"Dad, can I ask you a few questions?"

"Fire away," he replied, cheerfully. A good night's sleep had
helped him to regain his composure.

"Who is the Mr. Hanson I've heard you mention to mum?"

"Why do you ask?"

"Well, you said last night that you would tell me about him
some time."

"I met him long before I met your mother, in a pub actually,"
said Mr. Denvers. "I was unemployed, and he owned his own
building firm here in London. We talked for a while, and he
seemed to like me. He wanted someone to take his place when
he retired and he gave me a job. He became like a father to
me, and within five years, he offered me a partnership in the
firm, which I accepted. His own son had no interest in the
building trade, and I think John was bitterly disappointed. He
was a man of few words, but he was kind, and I shall never
forget what he did for me."

He paused, then told Rachel of Mr. Hanson's legacy from his
friend, Michael Drew, and how he had Michael's great-great
grandmother's will in his possession. "It mentions a fifth ruby
necklace which went missing in her day," said Mr. Denvers.
"John Hanson left it with Michael's will in a drawer in his
office. It states that if the necklace ever came to light, it should
follow the line of descent. In other words, it should be given to
the oldest remaining member of the family, to be passed on. If
there were no descendants living, it would become the

property of the person who discovered it. She must have hoped that it would be found in the lifetimes of her children, then it would have been easy to prove ownership due to all the publicity about its loss. The last clause must have been put in to prevent the necklace being claimed by the state."

Rachel was stunned. They were the same people. She'd spoken to them in a time before she was born!

"Would the will still be legal today, dad?" I mean, if anyone found the necklace now?"

"Yes," replied her father, smiling. "But I should think it was found and kept by someone many years ago. A millionaire in London bought the other four ruby necklaces from John Hanson. "I believe he still has them."

Rachel was deep in thought for a moment, then she asked breathlessly, "did Mr. Hanson have any family apart from his son?"

"Yes, he had a wife called Doris, whom I met a few times, and a daughter called Emily. I never met her." Rachel felt the colour drain from her face while her father was speaking.

"Are you alright love, you look a bit white?"

"I'm fine, dad. Where are the Hansons now?"

"They were all killed in a plane crash, while flying out to Switzerland on holiday," he replied. "That's why I own the firm — or did until today," he added bitterly.

Rachel felt numb. "I think I'll go upstairs and lie down dad. I do feel a bit tired."

"Okay love. I'll bring you a drink later on."

"Thanks," said Rachel.

In her bedroom, she threw herself on the bed and cried for the Hansons, clutching the green umbrella in despair. 'They're alive in the war, aren't they?' she thought, as the umbrella started to vibrate in her hands, turning once again on the floor. As the scene began to change, Rachel noticed the clock, and the time at 11.30, before it vanished with the rest of her bedroom.

When the spinning stopped, she looked down in astonishment at the long shawl, black ankle-length dress and the thick-soled leather shoes. In one hand, she was carrying a black leather bag and ahead of her was a stone building with a grey pillared porchway and wrought iron gates. Across the street, she could see a street vendor, dressed in shabby clothes of a bygone age, selling oysters from his cart.

"Oysters penny a lot," he called, "oysters penny a lot."

A ragged urchin came along the pavement and she asked him what city she was in and what year it was.

"Liverpool, 1860," he sniffed, wiping a grimy hand across his mouth. "Ere, where've you been then?" he asked, leering up at her face with dark, hard eyes. A horse pulling a hansom cab rushed between them, and Rachel stepped back in dismay.

'Victorian Liverpool,' she thought, astonished. Coming to a quick decision, she walked towards the house with the iron gates.

CHAPTER SIX

TALKING TO LUCY

Rachel's knock was muffled by the sound of the carriages, and it was several minutes before she heard footsteps within. The door swung open to reveal a large stout woman with a round ruddy face, wearing a black floor-length dress, mob cap and white apron. Under her arm she carried a mixing bowl.

"Yes, what do you want?" she snapped, then peering at Rachel more closely, "Oh, you'll be the new parlour maid we were expecting from the agency. You'd best come in." She held the door open and waited. Rachel hesitated, then decided to go along with the idea. "Come on," snapped the woman, impatiently, "I can't stand here all day. I've got to cook the evening meal for the family." Rachel walked into the kitchen and saw the cooking range with a fire burning on either side of two wooden doors, and a long wooden table in the centre of the room. "I hope you're better than the last maid we had," said the woman coldly. "She couldn't do anything right. My name's Mrs. Burns, by the way. I'm the cook. What are you known as?" She told the woman her name. "Well Rachel," said Mrs. Burns firmly. "In the absence of the mistress of the house, you will answer to me for all that you do. Do you understand?" She glared fiercely at Rachel, her eyes glinting.

"I understand," said Rachel, apprehensively. A door banged in the passage and two younger girls came into the kitchen. They were both wearing print dresses, with white aprons and caps. One girl was carrying a feather duster and was taller than her companion. "Don't make so much noise, girls," said the cook, irritably.

"Sorry, Mrs. Burns," said the taller girl.

The cook frowned. "This is Annie, the housemaid, Rachel,"
she said, pointing to the dark-haired girl with the duster.
Rachel looked into her kindly eyes and felt warmed. "… and
this is Letty, the under-housemaid." Rachel couldn't have
said why she felt uncomfortable when she looked at Letty. She
seemed pleasant enough. Perhaps she had imagined the

shiftiness in her eyes. "Rachel is our new parlour maid. Take her up to her room, Annie, while she puts on her cap and apron, then I want you both down here. There's work to be done."

The two girls had just walked into the hall, when the front door opened, and in ran a laughing girl and a boy, dripping wet. The boy was dark-haired, and wore a long-belted tweed jacket and trousers, and the girl had auburn ringlets, and wore a long coat which was closed to the waist and open at the bottom. She began to shake something in her hands, producing a shower of raindrops which glistened in the light from the gas lamp as they fell to the floor. Rachel caught her breath. In the girl's hand was the green umbrella! "Come on," said Annie to Rachel. "Don't stare. It's Miss Lucy and her brother Simon, the master's son and daughter." When they moved, the girl saw them, and asked to be introduced. Annie told her who Rachel was, and Lucy clapped her hands together withglee. "I'm so glad you've come, Rachel," said Lucy Happily. "I need a maid to help me take off these awful wet clothes. Will you come to my room when you've put your uniform on?"

"But she's the parlour maid, Miss Lucy," said Annie, frightened. "Mrs. Burns will be terribly cross."

"Oh bother Mrs. Burns, Annie. I'll take care of her," said Lucy.Annie's lips tightened to a hard line as she took Rachel up several flights of stairs to the top floor. They went into a small bedroom containing a bed, a dressing table, chest chair and cabinet.

"This is your room," said Annie, kindly. Rachel put down her bag, took off her shawl and put on the mob cap and apron which were lying on the bed. Glancing in a mirror, she chuckled inwardly at her hair, which was swept back in a bun, before following Annie to Lucy's bedroom on the next floor. Inside, Lucy was sitting at a dressing table, combing out her ringlets, surrounded by oppressive mahogany furniture and heavily draped windows.

"Will you help me undress please, Rachel?" asked Lucy charmingly, gracing Rachel with a dazzling smile. "I feel soaked through." Rachel reached over and managed to undo the hooks and eyes down the centre back of the bodice and Lucy slipped the lacy sleeves off her shoulders and pulled the dress over her head. Off came several stiffened petticoats, followed by a chemise with stays at the top, and cream, knee-length knickers. Rachel's eyes widened. "Anyone would think you had never seen these types of garments before, Rachel," laughed Lucy. "Your face is a picture."

"I'm, sorry," said Rachel. "I didn't mean to stare. Do you want me to help you with anything else, miss?"

"Yes, you can pass me the robe by the door and brush my hair," said Lucy grandly.

"Yes miss." Rachel thought her rather spoilt but likeable, so she played the game, but was worried when she caught a troubled expression on Lucy's face, reflected in the mirror. Is there something wrong, Miss Lucy?"

"I was thinking of a nasty experience I had a few weeks ago," replied Lucy.

"Would you like to talk about it?" asked Rachel, addressing her as an equal.

Lucy looked up sharply. "Yes, I would," she said, relieved. "You know, any other maid would have kept silent, aware of my higher station in life, but you're different, Rachel. I like you." Rachel understood and smiled. She brushed Lucy's hair with long smooth strokes.

"My father," began Lucy, "had arranged to have five ruby necklaces made, to form a collection. He is a great admirer of beautiful objects, and loves gems of all kinds." Rachel stiffened and held the brush in mid-air. "The first one," continued Lucy, "was to be given to my mother. My father told only my brother Simon and me what he was doing." She turned round and saw Rachel's shocked expression. "What's the matter?" asked Lucy, alarmed.

"What is your father's name, Miss Lucy?" asked Rachel in a whisper.

"Mr. Drew. Mr. Jonathon Drew," said Lucy. "He made a fortune with the trading ships we own in Liverpool docks. I thought you would have known that already. Aren't you feeling well?"

Rachel was astounded. 'I'm actually waiting on the daughter of Michael Drew's great-great-grandfather,' she thought. 'What would Emily say to that?' She felt an anxious pair of eyes upon her and began to brush Lucy's hair in a frenzy of excitement.

"Not so hard, Rachel!" cried Lucy, wincing. "You'll have my head off."

"Oh, I'm sorry," said Rachel. "Please carry on."

"Well," sighed Lucy. "Papa, Simon and I went to pick up the first necklace, which was ready. The others hadn't been completed at the time. When we were coming out of the jewellers with the necklace, something horrid happened. We were crossing the road to our carriage when a hansom cab came out of nowhere and thundered towards us. Papa and Simon ran out of the way, but I couldn't move. I was rooted to the spot with terror."

"How awful," gasped Rachel, enthralled. "What happened next?"

"A girl ran out of a crowd of people and pushed me out of the way," said Lucy, quietly.

"What happened to her?" asked Rachel.

"The horse caught her a glancing blow and knocked her to the ground unconscious," said Lucy. She twisted her hands anxiously. "I remember looking into the eyes of the cab driver as he charged past. They were evil. I'm sure it wasn't an accident, Rachel." She grabbed Rachel's arm tightly, and said in a hushed voice. "Someone tried to kill us. I'm certain of that. He didn't even stop."

Rachel was appalled. She now felt sure that she was here to protect Lucy in some way. "How did you help the girl who saved your life, Miss Lucy?" asked Rachel, quietly.

"We brought her back here with a doctor. He said that with rest and care, she would recover, so we nursed her here for a week. She would tell us nothing about her life or where she lived, but I noticed she was interested in my umbrella. She couldn't take her eyes off it. She had lovely brown hair and a funny turned-up nose." Lucy sighed and looked puzzled.

Rachel's agitation was so great by now that she felt she had to ask the next question. "Did she give you her name?" she asked.

"Emily," answered Lucy, softly.

Rachel closed her eyes and tried to collect her thoughts, which were racing around in her head. 'So, the umbrella brought Emily back to help Lucy too. I wonder where she is now.'

As if she had heard the question, Lucy said, "About a week ago, she disappeared. We searched the house for her, and put up notices all over town. No one had seen her. She just vanished."

'She's gone back to her own time,' thought Rachel, disappointed. 'I would have loved to have spoken to her again.'

Her mind focused. "Have you owned the umbrella long, Miss Lucy? It's a lovely colour."

"Only a month," replied Lucy. "My father bought it for my birthday. They're quite the fashion now, you know."

'So Lucy is the first owner,' thought Rachel. "Have I brushed your hair enough?" she asked.

"Yes, thank you, Rachel. You can go back to your duties now," answered Lucy, softly.

"Thank you, Miss Lucy," said Rachel politely. I know I'm only the parlour maid, but if you ever need a friend, you can count on me."

"That means a lot to me, Rachel," said Lucy, warmly. The gloom disappeared from her face. "My brother and I are going to stay with some friends overnight, tomorrow. Would you like to come with us as my maid?" asked Lucy, eagerly.

"If it's allowed," said Rachel, doubtfully.

"Oh, I'll fix it with papa," cried Lucy, delighted. "He seems stern, but I can usually get round him. He thinks the world of Simon and me." Rachel gave a wry smile and closed the door. In the kitchen, downstairs, she could hear raised voices. The loudest belonged to Mrs. Burns.

"She's only been here a few minutes and she thinks she's a lady's maid, better than us all," shrilled Mrs. Burns hysterically. "I'll fix that one. Wait till she comes down."

"Give the wretch what she deserves," said Letty, maliciously. Rachel took a deep breath and pushed open the door. "What would you like me to do now, Mrs. Burns?" she asked, haughtily. She received the shocked stare of Mrs. Burns without flinching. The only sound came from a large pan of potatoes, bubbling on the range. Mrs. Burns screwed up her heavy red jowls and her eyes narrowed to slits in her pudgy face.

"I've got my eyes on you, my girl," she said threateningly to Rachel. "Step out of line once – just once mind- and you'll be out of that door before you know what's hit you. My word carries weight here with the mistress. Do you understand?"

"Perfectly," said Rachel, trying to control her inner shaking. "Only I'm not really a maid," she added, thinking it was time to make a stand. "I was lost and came here for help. You insisted I had come to fill the vacancy. Should I set the table for tea?" Mrs Burns went white with shock.

"How dare you lie to me," she hissed, menacingly. The veins in her neck swelled to twice their normal size. "Of course, you're the parlour maid. You can't escape that easily. Annie, take Lady Muck here into the dining room and show her where the cutlery is kept. Then come back and help me. Letty, get that sauce prepared and be quick about it."

In the dining room, Annie showed Rachel where everyone sat, and helped her to set the places. "Don't worry," she said kindly to Rachel. "Mrs. Burns can have her way with the mistress, but not with the master. Serve each dish as you bring it in. There's only four of them. Mr. and Mrs. Drew, Miss Lucy and Master Simon. The governess, Miss Flint, has her meal upstairs."

Time passed quickly from then on, as Rachel laid out plates and glasses. She turned up the gas lamps as Annie had shown her. When the dinner gong sounded, she was joined by a portly gentleman with a bald head. He introduced himself as Mr. Hartley, the butler. When the family had settled, and Mr. Drew had said grace, they began to serve the first dish. Rachel watched the butler serving and tried to copy everything he did. She leaned over Mrs. Drew's slender shoulder with a portion of meat, and looked into a pair of gentle green eyes. She glanced at Rachel and smiled.

Mr. Drew stroked his side-whiskers and moustache as he studied Rachel. "So, you are the new parlour maid?" he said, gruffly. "I trust you will be happy here."

"I'm sure I will, sir," said Rachel, demurely. She served more vegetables to Lucy.

"Papa, can –," began Lucy.

"Lucy!" barked Mr. Drew, cutting her off in mid-sentence. "Children should be seen and not heard at the table. Wait till you are spoken to." Lucy looked downcast until she saw the twinkle in her father's eye. After dinner, Mr. Drew retired to the study to smoke a cigar, while Lucy and Simon followed their mother into the dining room.

Rachel stared at the size of Mrs. Drew's crinoline dress, which spread out around her when she walked. It was late that night when Rachel, Annie and Letty finally dragged themselves up the stairs to the top floor and crawled into bed.

At four thirty in the morning, she was awakened by Annie and promptly went back to sleep, thinking it was a joke. Annie shook her again and told her to get dressed as all the servants must rise early. She blearily obeyed and went downstairs in a stupor. 'What an awful time Victorian servants must have had,' she thought, as Letty pushed past carrying two buckets of water for the family to wash in. There was no running water upstairs. After breakfast Lucy disappeared into the schoolroom with Miss Flint for her morning's lessons, and after she had finished she ran into the dining room and told Rachel that she could come with herself and her brother that night. Her father had given permission early that morning.

"I'm so glad I've finished my lessons for today," sighed Lucy. "What do you study, Miss Lucy?" asked Rachel curiously. "Oh, French, history geography, arithmetic, drawing singing and needlework. Ugh!" replied Lucy, grimacing. "You don't know what you're missing." Rachel laughed. She was pleased that she would be with Lucy that night. As she approached the kitchen, she heard Mr. Drew speaking, "- and so, Mrs. Burns, for this night only, I am allowing Rachel to go with my daughter and son. I'm sure you know how nervous Miss Lucy is after that unfortunate accident. She will feel better having another companion. Annie can wait on table until they return," he said firmly.

"Yes, sir." said Mrs. Burns, deflated. Mr. Drew walked past Rachel in the hall, and she entered the kitchen. "You little sneak," snapped Mrs. Burns. "I'll finish off your airs and graces when you get back." Letty could barely suppress a look of gloating triumph as she stared boldly at Rachel, while Annie's gaze was one of open admiration. Rachel remained silent.

In the evening, Rachel went upstairs and opened her black bag. She hadn't done so the night before because she had been tired. Even then, she had been amused by the underwear she had on, especially the knickers and black worsted stocking. Now, she saw that inside the bag was an identical change of clothing, and included was a pair of stays. She suppressed a giggle and made a mental note not to wear them.

When they were ready, Simon Lucy and Rachel went out to the carriage which was standing in the drive. The horse paced one foot, while snorting hot steamy breath into the thick swirling fog.

Simon looked up at the driver, curiously. "Where's James tonight?" he asked. "He's our usual driver. I've never seen you before."

"He's ill, master Simon," he replied, in a muffled voice. "I'm taking his place tonight. Jump in."

"Nothing serious, I hope?" asked Simon, worried.

"No, just a bad chest," muttered the man.

"Do you know where we are going?" asked Simon.

"Yes, I know that alright," he replied, adjusting his top hat ceremoniously. When they were all inside, the carriage set off through the gate and down the road. The fog became thicker, and the three travellers were uneasy. They could hear the muffled hoof-beats of the horse, but apart from that, they existed in a dead silent world which went on endlessly.

"How can he see where we're going?" asked Simon, anxiously.

"Aren't we a long time getting there?" asked Lucy.

"I'll shout to the driver," said Simon, manfully. "Don't worry girls, I'll take care of you." He poked his head through the window and called, "hey driver, where are we?" No answer. He shouted again. Nothing. Lucy was getting agitated.

"Let's jump out," she cried, making for the door.

"No!" said Rachel, firmly, holding Lucy's arm in a strong grip, as the carriage came to a standstill.

Rachel felt cruel hands thrust a gag into her mouth while her arms were tied and a blindfold put over her eyes. The carriage set off once more into the murky night.

"Now's our chance," said Simon, throwing open the door. Three strong men jumped inside, and Lucy let out a piercing scream.

CHAPTER SEVEN

KIDNAPPED

The carriage rolled on, turning numerous times into unknown streets, as they struggled, stiff and sore from their bonds. At last, they came to a halt, and were led outside and down a flight of cold stone steps and through a door. Rachel faltered and slipped, and powerful hands yanked her upright. They had their bonds untied, and the blindfolds removed, causing them to blink rapidly, in the sudden light which came from an oil lamp on a wooden table. The dank stone walls were covered with a green, foul-smelling slime, and above their heads was a high basement window, made up of several panes of glass. One pane was missing.

"Don't scream," said a rough, menacing male voice behind them, "cos no-one can 'ear you. Sit on the floor by the wall and be quiet."

They huddled in a corner, while the three men shuffled over to the far side of the room.

"What do you think they are going to do to us?" whispered Lucy, frightened.

"I don't know," answered Rachel, "but did you see the tall one? His mouth was awful. It was just a red slit."

"Yes, but the big fat one looks as if he could squeeze the life out of someone. Look at his hands." They all peered into the half-light across the room. His huge gnarled hands were clenched hard.

"Well, I don't trust any of them," said Lucy, shaking. "He'd better not come near me. She looked over to the third man who was glancing furtively round the room. "Perhaps I feel sorry for the small man at the end," she said, relenting.

"What for?" asked Rachel, shocked.

"He's bent over double and walks with a limp. I don't think he wants to be here at all."

"That makes two of us," said Simon derisively. "I don't think we should waste too much sympathy on any of them." Lucy looked downcast and Rachel squeezed her hand sympathetically. "I wonder what they did to your coachman?" she asked, worried. "I hope they haven't hurt him."

"So do I," said Lucy.

"They've probably knocked him out and tied him up somewhere," said Simon. "Poor old James. You know, I didn't like the look of that new driver, when we first saw him."

"Well I wish you had said something then," said Lucy.

"I wonder who the driver was?" asked Rachel.

"One of their evil mates, no doubt," said Simon, dourly. "They're obviously from the lower classes. Sorry, Rachel, I didn't mean that to be an insult to you." He glanced at her sheepishly.

She looked amused. "I'll forgive you, master Simon."

"Look out," whispered Lucy, hurriedly. "They're coming over."

The tall man emerged into the light, and Lucy gasped and shrank back. Simon put his arm protectively round her shoulders.

"So, you have recognised me, Lucy," he said, coldly.

"You're the man who tried to run us down in the street with a hansom cab," said Lucy, shaking.

"That's right," he replied, coldly. "We have all had a little chat and have decided to let you in on the game. My name is Mike," he said. "This is Sam. Don't upset Sam, my dears. He's rather jumpy. His hands sometimes get a little itchy to be round a soft pliant neck " Enjoying the fear in their eyes, he continued. "This is Jed, our man with a limp, who had an accident with a train.

"Why have you brought us here?" asked Rachel, abruptly, trying to keep her voice steady. Sam laughed mirthlessly, and she shivered.

"Unfortunately, Lucy, I haven't got what I want yet," said Mike, ignoring Rachel's question.

"What do you want?" asked Simon, angrily.

"The ruby necklace," replied Mike. A shocked silence filled the room.

"How did you know about that?"

"We had a spy in your house," he answered, amused.

"Who?" asked Simon.

"Letty," said Mike, triumphantly. "She's my sister." Rachel remembered the shiftiness she had seen in Letty's eyes yesterday, and her malicious comment to Mrs. Burns. 'I was right about Letty,' she thought, sadly. Mike looked at Rachel. "Pity you had to come out tonight girl," he said.

Rachel glared. "Where's the Drew's coachman?" she asked.

"Oh, he'll be alright," said Mike, flippantly. "Our man is on his way back to the house with the coach now. When Jed delivers the ransom note, it will explain where he can be found and untied." Jed shuffled his feet uneasily on the floor, and seemed dejected. His sunken green eyes took on a hunted expression.

`He's the weak link`, thought Rachel.

"Now, I think we'll get down to business," said Mike, briskly. "I'll take your umbrella Lucy. It figures in our plans, you see." She stared at him in horror, and put the umbrella behind her back. Mike laughed for the first time and Sam made a grab for Lucy, holding her by the throat. Simon leapt to her defence but was flung away. "You can let her go now," said Mike. Sam released his grip and took the umbrella. Lucy fell backwards, gasping for breath.

"You inhuman devils," cried Simon, holding Lucy's head, while Rachel rubbed her throat. "You'll pay for this when my father hears of it."

"That, my dears," said Mike, calmly, "was a demonstration of what Sam will do if you don't obey my requests immediately. Now sit still."

They were tied up to three hooks by the damp wall, while the kidnappers sat round the table. The light from the lamp threw huge grotesque shadows onto the wall behind, and lit up their evil features. Mike was writing on a piece of paper.

"Are you alright, Miss Lucy?" asked Rachel, anxiously.

"Yes, I think so," said Lucy in a rasping voice. "I've got a sore throat though."

"We've got to stop them," whispered Simon.

"I don't know how," said Rachel, scathingly.

"I'll think of something," said Simon. "By the way Lucy, how did Letty know about the necklace?"

"She was polishing furniture in the morning room, when papa told us he was picking it up that day," said Lucy, hoarsely. Her voice gave a loud rasp as she tried to force the words out. The men looked suspiciously in their direction, then bent once more over the table.

"Did Letty hear anything about the other ruby necklaces?" asked Rachel.

"Not that I know of."

"Well, that's something anyway. I wonder why they wanted your umbrella."

"That's just what I would like to know."

Just then, Mike stood up and his shadow reached up the far wall and halfway across the ceiling. "Take this note, Jed, and put it through the Drew's letter box. Make sure you aren't seen, "he said, handing a folded piece of paper to the wiry man. Jed's hand hesitated halfway, drew back, then lunged forward and took it.

"I don't think Jed's as bad as the other two," whispered Rachel. "Mike is the obvious leader, the brains of the gang. Sam provides the muscle."

"They're all horrible," said Lucy, with hatred. "Look what that big ape did to me. Jed
could have stopped him."

They all fell silent as Mike and Sam left the room with the umbrella. Jed looked sheepish.

"Why are you doing this, Jed?" asked Rachel, quickly.

"I have to," he replied, warily.

"Why?"

"Because I don't want to be laughed at all my life, and looked down on. With money, I'll be respected, and people won't care what I look like," cried Jed, passionately.

"But you are doing wrong, Jed," said Rachel, reproachfully.

"I'm sorry, really I am," said Jed, hurriedly. "I'll try to make sure they don't harm you. I'm only in it for the money." Rachel could say no more, as the other two men came back into the room. "Off you go then, Jed," said Mike. "Try to be quick." Jed threw a contrite look at Rachel, before sidling out of the door. "Now it's my turn," said Mike, holding the green umbrella in one hand. "I shan't be long, Sam. Take care of our guests while I'm gone." Mike disappeared through the door, leaving them alone with the giant with the huge hands. Sam checked all their bonds, then lurched over to the table, to drink from an open bottle. For some time, he sat swilling it back, gradually slumping over the wooden surface, fast asleep.

"They're not going to let us live, now that we know their plans, are they?" asked Rachel.

"No they're not," answered Simon, hotly. "Try to get the ropes off girls, while we can." Sam began to snore loudly as they struggled in vain to free themselves. After a while, they heard two pairs of footsteps clatter down the stone staircase outside, and a key turn in the lock. Sam roused himself, as Mike and Jed walked in with the green umbrella.

"Well, Sam," said Mike, triumphantly. "We've got the necklace. Jed, you stay here and watch these kids. Sam, come with me into the next room. I want to talk to you." Sam got up from his chair rather unsteadily, and swayed out of the room behind Mike. The door closed with a bang.

CHAPTER EIGHT

IN THE CELLAR

"Get us out of here, Jed!" cried Simon, frantically.

"They'd kill me!" said Jed, terrified. "They're real mean. I can't do nothing."

"You could untie us," said Simon, eagerly, "while they're out of the room."

Jed ignored Simon's remark. He sidled over to the table and took some food out of a box.

"Here, have something to eat," he said, feeding them a piece of bread and fruit in turn. He walked to a chair and sat with his head in his hands.

"He's weakening, wondering what to do," whispered Rachel. "Would you like any food yourself, Jed?" she asked, warmly. "You look hungry too."

Jed's hands dropped to his knees and his head came up slowly, revealing pain filled eyes.

"No thanks," he said, dismally. "I couldn't eat nothing."

"Have you any family, Jed?" asked Rachel, eager to keep his attention.

"Not now," he sighed "Had a brother once, a few years older than me. We were orphans and they put us int'workhouse. I don't remember me mother and father. They died just after I was born. When we left the workhouse, Tom, me brother and me, went as navvies on t'railway. Always looked after me, did Tom. A train came loose from a siding we were working on one day. He was killed. I was crippled."

"I'm sorry, how terrible. Would your brother have approved of you doing this though, Jed?"

Jed's face twisted spasmodically and a tear edged its way down his cheek. "No, he wouldn't," said Jed, shamefaced. "Tom always taught me to walk the straight and narrow, no matter what. It wasn't easy for me when I lost Tom. I couldn't get another job and people stared at me int' street. I thought everyone had it in for me. Then I met Mike and Sam." He shifted his gaze and looked down at the floor.

"I just wanted some money to put me on me feet again, but I don't want no part in killing people. I— I suppose I've been silly really," he

continued, shakily. There was a short silence, and then he said, "I'll

help you escape, miss. You don't need to say no more."

"Thank you Jed," said Rachel, relieved.

"About time too," snapped Simon.

Jed went over to Lucy, who stared at him with tearful eyes. "I had no idea people lived like that," she sobbed. "I feel so sorry for you Jed."

"Do you miss?" asked Jed, astonished. "Don't waste your pity on me. I just want to be accepted."

The ropes on Lucy's wrists wouldn't budge, and he had no more luck with Rachel and Simon. Sam laughed in the next room and they froze.

"We'll have to work fast, Jed, they won't stay in there forever. Have you

got a knife?" asked Rachel.

"No," said Jed, thoughtfully, "but Sam has."

"That's no good," said Simon, scathingly. "You can hardly go and ask him to lend you his knife while you untie us."

"Don't be so cruel Simon," cried Lucy, passionately.

"Alright, but what do we do now?"

Rachel's eye caught sight of a jagged piece of glass on the basement window.

"Wouldn't that be sharp enough if you could break it off, Jed?" she asked, hopefully.

Jed followed her gaze. "It might, miss," he answered, enthusiastically pulling over a chair and climbing up. He wrenched the glass back and forth while the others held their breath. Suddenly, it came loose with a loud jarring sound, and they all looked fearfully towards the door. There was no movement.

"Right," said Jed. "Let's get on with it." He cut the strands on Rachel's wrists and soon she was free. She rubbed her hands to ease the numbness, while she listened at the door, as he sliced the glass over the rope on Lucy's wrists. One strand snapped. Then two, three. She was free.

"Thank you," said Lucy, relieved.

"Hear owt?" Jed asked, before starting on Simon.

"Not yet," answered Rachel, pushing her ear against the wooden door. All they could hear was the harsh rasping sound of the glass on the rope, until Simon too was free. Rachel opened the door slowly and the sound of mumbled conversation drifted in from the room on the other side of the dark smelly passageway.

"Why isn't the door locked?" whispered Lucy.

"They think I'm guarding you," said Jed, in a hushed voice.

"Where are we?" whispered Simon.

"In a deserted street, 'bout six miles from your home," whispered Jed.

"Shut the door miss. We can't talk wi'it open. We've got to get out of here now."

"Just tell me why there is no-one living here, and how you got hold of the keys," asked Simon, urgently.

"A nasty illness broke out, so they had to evacuate everybody," said Jed.

"What illness?" asked Simon, alarmed.

"Scarlet fever," said Jed, irritably.

"Scarlet fever!" they all gasped.

"It's alright," said Jed, "the doctor who moved everyone had the buildings fumi…fumi…,"
"Fumigated?" asked Rachel, relieved."
"Yes, that's it," answered Jed.
"Letty read it int'papers. She knew the people who lived 'ere and they let 'er have the keys."
"Letty again," said Lucy, scornfully. "Come on, let's get out of here."
"Right," said Jed. "When we go out, turn left, walk up the stairs and open the door at the top, quietly! Miss Rachel, you go first, Miss Lucy next, then you, master Simon. I'll go last."
 "What about my umbrella?" asked Lucy.
"Leave it," said Simon, sternly. Rachel opened the door and they all walked slowly in single file to the base of the stairs. Quietly, feeling their way in the darkness, they inched their way up the steps. Rachel put her hand on the knob of the door at the top and was about to turn it, when a door opened downstairs and out came Mike and Sam, silhouetted by the light.
"I thought I heard something," said Mike, looking up to where Jed was standing. "Shall we all go back inside?" Jed and Simon put up a struggle, but they were overpowered.
"Run for it girls!" shouted Simon, bravely.
Rachel opened the door and came face to face with the driver of their carriage.
"I shouldn't do that," he said, menacingly "Shall we go down?"
"Nicely timed Jack," said Mike. As the man moved forward, Rachel stooped and dived under his arm into the empty street. The fog had cleared but it was half dark and the gas lamps weren't lit along the pavement. Instinct made her run to the right, but she was hindered by her long clothing. Hearing heavy footsteps behind, she looked back to see Jack the driver gaining speed, but she kept up her run until her heart was bursting.

Somewhere to the left, a voice said, "Quick, over here!" and she dived into a dark alleyway. Two urchins, hiding in a doorway, pulled her inside as she collapsed in a heap on the doorstep, and began to pour out her story.

"Please tell the police," she said, urgently. "Go quickly, while there's still time. Leave me, I can't run any further. Tell them to go to the cellar with the lamp." The urchins fled into the night, as Jack turned the corner and ran past Rachel's hideaway. She huddled further into the darkness and gathered her dress around her. The footsteps receded and then stopped. She listened intently, then they started again and began to come closer. 'He's coming back!' she thought in alarm. He stopped opposite the doorway and Rachel could see the whites of his eyes as he looked searchingly around. As he started to move off, Rachel's foot, which was balanced precariously on the step, fell with a thud onto the ground below. The man hesitated, then began to walk towards her. Rachel made a dash for it, but he caught her by the arm and threw her over his shoulder.

"Got her," said Jack, as he put her down onto the floor in the cellar with the others, and tied her up again.

"Good work," said Mike. "Come and join us Jack. We need to talk." The men whispered together, while Rachel told her story to Lucy and Simon.

"But will they be in time?" asked Lucy, when Rachel had finished.

"They might not go to the police," said Simon, gloomily.

"I'm sure they will," said Rachel, optimistically.

"It's all up for me now," said Jed, downcast.

Rachel sighed. "We'll vouch for you. They won't be too hard on you when we've had our say." After some time, Mike, Sam and Jack came over.

"Right men, you know what to do. Get on with it." Sam brought out a long pointed silver knife which shone as it caught the light from the oil lamp. They all gasped with fear.

His eyes narrowed to evil slits as he bent over Rachel and lifted his arm high, ready to strike.

CHAPTER NINE

PAST PRESENT AND FUTURE

The distant sound of screaming and the pounding feet on the stairs roused her enough to push away while Sam was distracted. Four policemen, each carrying oil lanterns burst through the door, and manhandled the three astonished kidnappers while she trembled with relief, watching their chimney pot hats wave up and down with the struggle. Standing in the doorway, with expressions of sheer delight on their faces, were the two urchins Rachel had spoken to when she escaped. They looked down and saw her.

"Cor, are you alright, miss?" asked the taller boy.

"We figured you must have been caught again, as there was no sign of you down the alley. Looks as though we're just in time." He sniffed loudly and jumped out of the way as two policemen, struggling to take the knife from Sam, backed into him.

"Yes, I'm alright now," said Rachel. Her legs felt weak.

"Thanks for saving our lives. What were you doing down that alley?"

"Oh, me and Tim always sleep down in the basement there. We've no home, and the people who left it empty, forgot to lock up. You're real lucky we were there, miss."

"I know," said Rachel.

"Look!" cried Lucy, excitedly. "They've knocked the knife out of Sam's hand.

They've got him pinned down."

"Jack's broken free!" cried Rachel, as the driver wrenched himself away and dived for the door. Tim, the urchin, put out a foot and Jack sprawled headlong and knocked himself out cold on the stone floor. Tim winked and rubbed his hands together with glee.

"Thank you, young man," said the policeman. "That was quick thinking. Where's the fourth kidnapper?" He glanced at Jed and let out a long sigh.

"So, they tied you up too, did they?"

Jed stared dismally at his feet.

"He tried to help us escape," said Rachel, protectively. "That must help in his defence, mustn't it?" She looked at him pleadingly.

"Well, it should do. We'll have to see about that at the trial." He turned to the urchins. "Hey, you two, how about cutting these people free while we take out the prisoners. Don't undo the man though. I'll tackle him." He disappeared through the door, dragging Jack with him, and was followed by his colleagues pushing Sam and Mike. The elder boy picked up Sam's knife from the floor and when he cut the ropes, they all sighed with relief and stood up to stretch their aching limbs. A few minutes later, a policeman came back and untied Jed, and they all walked eagerly towards the stairs. Simon and Lucy were avidly explaining who they were and why they'd been kidnapped.

"Just a minute," said Lucy, suddenly. "Where's my umbrella?"

"I'll get it for you Lucy," said Rachel, kindly. "They must have left it in the other room. You all go up and I'll join you in a moment."

"Thank you Rachel," said Lucy, relieved. "I must admit that I want to get out of here as soon as possible and see dear mama and papa again. They must be so worried."

Rachel pushed open the door of the other room and found the umbrella with the help of an oil lamp, but as she bent down, it jumped onto its point and started to spin. 'Here we go again,' she thought, as the room began to revolve and change.

She blinked and gazed around at the familiar objects in her bedroom, with a sense of relief. 'What will they think has happened to me?' she asked herself. 'I suppose Emily must have felt the same in the war. They might think I'm a ghost.' The umbrella lay beside her on the bed and she nervously touched the handle. It remained still. The sunshine streamed through the window and made a patchwork of light and shade on the bedspread and her clothes. She knew without looking at the clock that no time had passed here in the present but she glanced at the hands just to make sure. It was eleven thirty. So much had happened, that she was finding it difficult to remember what she had been doing before her journey. Then she recalled the conversation with her father about the Hansons. Someone knocked on the door.

"Yes, who is it?" shouted Rachel, startled out of her reverie.

"It's me love," answered her father. "I've brought you some orange juice. Can I come in?"

"Oh yes dad," cried Rachel, throwing open the door excitedly. "It's so nice to see you."

"It's nice to see you too. We only saw each other a few moments ago though," he said, with a touch of his old humour. "Are you feeling better now?"

"Better?" asked Rachel, puzzled. Then she remembered. "Oh yes, much better thank you." She took the drink from her father's hand and sat on the bed, looking up at his twinkling eyes. "Dad, when will we have to sell the house?" she asked, quietly.

"As soon as possible," he replied, heavily. "I had meant to spare you this, but I'll tell you now. I've just this moment rung the estate agent, and a man is coming to value it on Monday while you're at school." Rachel put down the glass and stretched her arms around her father's neck, offering what comfort she could. Her possessions didn't mean so much now.

"I'll have to go down," he said, obviously cheered by Rachel's affection. "I have some paper work to do."

"Okay," I'll see you later. I think I'll stay up here and read for a while."

After he'd gone, she felt much stronger and calmer, and began to be more and more curious about the meaning of her adventures in the past. 'How does it all tie in with me? Can Emily, Lucy and Simon help us in the present? I must know, umbrella, please.' It lay still. She spent some time on her phone, researching the Second World War and Victorian England, realising how amazing it was to have lived herself in those times.

Somehow, Rachel got through the rest of her weekend and on Monday, she went to school. The day dawned wet and cloudy, and she took the umbrella with her, half expecting another trip into the past, to explain everything. But it was a normal day. She felt though, that the umbrella was waiting, and as she carried it through the streets, she could have sworn that it was excited. All her friends took turns parading round the playground, holding it over their heads, while the dark heavy sky looked sombrely down. They were all upset to hear about her father's firm, and Rachel felt even sadder to think she would probably have to leave her school and move elsewhere.

On the way home, she stopped in a deserted park and sat down on a bench in a clearing, to think. The rain had stopped a few hours earlier and the sun threw warm rays down between the scudding clouds. Suddenly, she became aware of someone. A tall dark-haired girl, wearing a mackintosh and jeans, was standing nearby and watching her intently. Her eyes kept moving sharply to the umbrella and then back again, then darting round the park in confusion.

"Would you like to sit down?" asked Rachel, in a friendly voice. "There's plenty of room."

"Er, well, yes, thank you," replied the girl. "I hope you didn't mind me staring at you like that. It must have seemed rude, only I was fascinated by your umbrella. I once owned one just like it."

"Did you!?" gasped Rachel, surprised. "Was it the same colour?"

"Yes, it was,"

"Where is it now?" asked Rachel, with mounting excitement.

"At home," replied the girl, uneasily.

"Where is your home?"

"I---I can't remember," said the girl, looking trapped. "Listen, can you tell me where we are exactly?"

"London, 2007," laughed Rachel. The girl looked shocked and twisted her hands together in panic.

"Your umbrella started spinning and brought you here from another time, didn't it?" asked Rachel, delighted.

"How did you know?" asked the girl, startled.

"I've had one or two adventures myself. When I saw how agitated you were, and how you took such and interest in my umbrella, I became suspicious. Then your following comments were a giveaway. Are you from the future? The umbrella always seems to bring people from their time into the past." The girl said that she was, and that her name was Janet. She wanted to hear about Rachel's time travels and sat spellbound while she talked. ----"and so the cellar changed and I was back in my bedroom at home," finished Rachel. Janet had listened to the kidnapping episode with growing disbelief and great excitement, and by now could barely suppress her feelings.

"I can tell you the end of that story, Rachel!" she cried. "It's been handed down in our family. You see, Jed was my great-great-great-grandfather!"

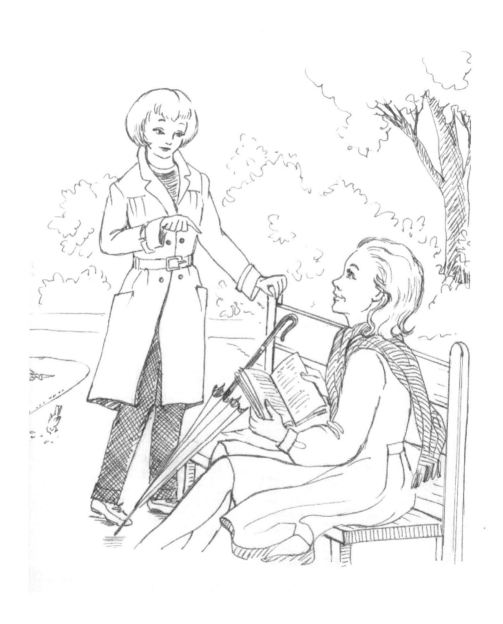

CHAPTER TEN

THE LOST NECKLACE

"This is incredible! cried Rachel. What did happen next then, Janet?"

Janet sat back on the bench and gazed far off into the distance. "When you disappeared," she began. "The authorities put out a search, but of course you were never found. The trial was a big one, and it caused quite a stir, because of the vanishing maid, and something else, which I'll come to in a minute. After Mr. Drew had received the ransom note, he took the ruby necklace from his safe at home and hurried out to the railway station cloakroom. The note said that he was to put the necklace in the stem of the umbrella, which was hollow. Letty, the under housemaid, had discovered that the top could be unscrewed, when she had been examining it admiringly in Lucy's bedroom one day." Rachel gasped, but didn't interrupt.

"Mike had arrived at the station beforehand, and after hanging the umbrella on a peg, had hidden behind a pillar. Mr. Drew came along and delivered the ransom. Then, following the note's instructions, he walked out of the station to a new rendezvous, where he should have been reunited with his children. He was told that if he informed anyone at all, they would be killed, and he was to destroy the note when he had read it. You know yourself Rachel, what happened when Mike returned. What you don't know, is that Mr. Drew had a weak heart. After waiting several hours for the release of his children, he suffered an attack and died."

"Oh, how awful," sighed Rachel, distressed.

"Yes, it was," agreed Janet. "I think he must have realized that the kidnappers had no intention of releasing Lucy and Simon. The stress killed him. He worshipped them. Of course, it was in all the papers and it shocked a lot of people." Janet looked thoughtful and was silent for a few moments. "Jed was sent to prison for his part in the crime, but as he did try to help you all escape, his sentence was less severe than the others. When he came out, he tried to trace the Drew family, to tell them where the necklace was hidden, but they had vanished. Apparently, Mrs. Drew had taken the children away after the trial and no-one knew their new address.

"Didn't Jed say where the necklace was?" asked Rachel, bewildered.

"He was afraid of Sam, Mike and Jack," said Janet, patiently. "He thought they would find him when they were released from prison and kill him."

"Yet he was prepared to risk their wrath by informing the Drew's when he did get out," said Rachel. "Was it because he thought they couldn't prove anything? I suppose Lucy could have found the necklace herself if she had unscrewed the top."

"Yes, that's it exactly," said Janet, pleased at Rachel's quick thinking.

"Only Jed never did know what happened after that. After working as a delivery man in a shop for some time, he put several advertisements in the local papers, asking for information about the Drew's whereabouts. But no-one answered. Jed realised that he wouldn't be safe when the other men came out of prison, so he moved out of Liverpool himself, and took a job in the Midlands. He met his wife there, a woman called Daisy Cooper, who was a maid in one of the big houses. He told her the story and their children passed it down, until my mother and father told me. From what we know, it seems that Daisy had a warm heart and put Jed on his feet. He adored her."

"I'm glad Jed made good in the end," said Rachel, warmly. "He wasn't all bad. I know that. Do you think the necklace was ever found, Janet?"

"Not by me," she replied. "I didn't know until now, that my umbrella was the same one that Jed and his friends had used in their plot. I received it when an old friend of my mother's died. As I knew it was Victorian, I wanted to see if the top would unscrew."

"Did it?" asked Rachel, curiously.

"Yes, it did,"

"There was nothing inside, so someone from the past must have removed it. Perhaps that someone is you, Rachel."

Rachel looked up in alarm. "Do you think so?" she asked, amazed. "I hadn't thought of that."

"There's only one way to find out. Undo the top," said Janet. Rachel didn't need telling twice. She twisted the handle hard, but she couldn't get it to budge an inch. "Did you have this trouble in your time?"

Janet nodded. "I had to ask my father to unscrew it. Here, let me try." Her face went red with the effort, but still it wouldn't move.

"Perhaps we'd better find a man in the park to help us then," said Rachel, scanning the deserted benches hopefully. "There's no-one around though."

"Let's walk down the road," suggested Janet. "We might find someone there."

They came out of the park and ran towards a long-haired youth wearing headphones. Shouting above the blare of music, they thrust the umbrella under his nose, but he glared at them disdainfully, then carried on down the street.

"Well, of all the bad-mannered louts," snapped Rachel, disappointed and annoyed.

"Never mind, Rachel," said Janet. Human nature doesn't change much. We still have people like that in my time. Look, there's someone else coming now."

Rachel charged off again with Janet in tow, and this time they were successful. A kindly older man did as he was asked. Although it took him a while, the handle finally moved and came off in his hand. He gave the pieces back to Rachel and smiled benevolently. Then he doffed his cap and strolled on. The girls went back into the park and Rachel

put her fingers inside the stem, moving them around as far
as they would go.

"There's nothing here!" she cried, with terrible
disappointment.

"The handle is quite long," said Janet. "Perhaps it's at the
bottom. Turn the umbrella upside down and shake it."
Rachel did this and for a second or two, nothing happened.
Then suddenly, out onto her lap fell the long-lost ruby
necklace. They both gasped. The sun's rays, much stronger
now, caught the gems and made them glint like red fire
She shrieked. "It's incredible."

"Now you'll be able to help your father save his firm," said
Janet, delighted.

"These should be yours Janet. I wouldn't have found them if
you hadn't told me." She looked worried.

"No, Rachel, You were meant to have the necklace, don't you
see? It had disappeared when I looked. The umbrella took
you back into the past and brought me here for this reason."

"Thanks Janet," she said, relieved. "Do you think I'll be the
old woman who owned the umbrella in the future?"

"Perhaps," answered Janet, whimsically. Then, more
emphatically, "I should say, probably."

"Will you tell me more about the future now?"

"You've already experienced the past which has been lived
before you," said Janet. Don't be in such a hurry about the
future Rachel. Live the present and take one day at a time."
Rachel thought of Emily Hanson and her family in the war
and their future fate, and she understood. From the corner of
her eye, she saw the umbrella jump up and begin to spin.
Janet shouted, "goodbye Rachel," and disappeared.

She gazed sadly at the space beside her on the bench and said
softly, "goodbye Janet." The umbrella had stopped spinning
and Rachel picked it up and hugged it to her in gratitude,
before walking home. She would have a lot of explaining to
do.

She let herself into the kitchen with a feeling of elation and pulled her mother into the living room, where her father was sitting hunched over the fire. Their lives would now change for the better, thanks to a special umbrella and the people linked to them in the past and the future. It had proved to Rachel that time was an illusion.

Printed in Great Britain
by Amazon